Victor packs

Story by Eliza Comodromos
Illustrations by Mark Weber

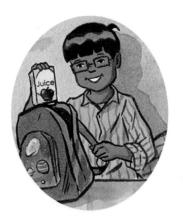

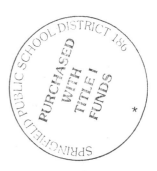

Dr. Judith Nadell, Series Editor

I pack my pencils.

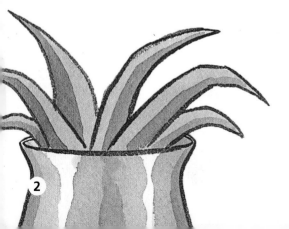

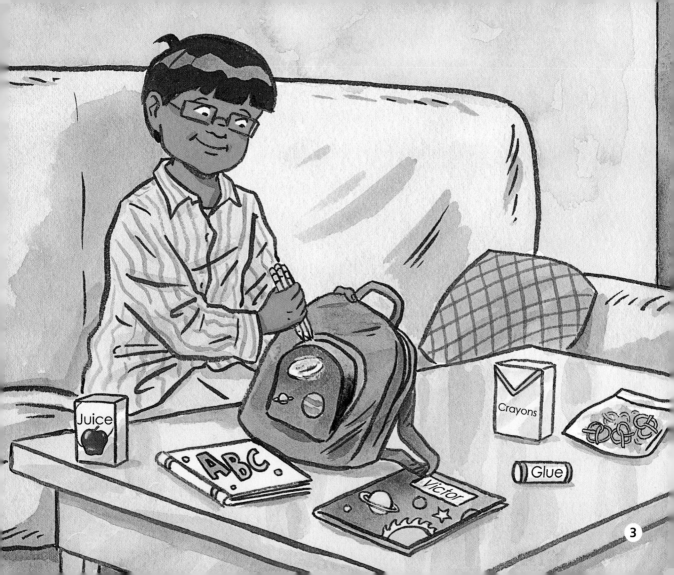

I pack my crayons.

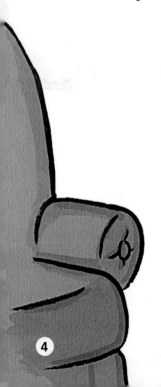

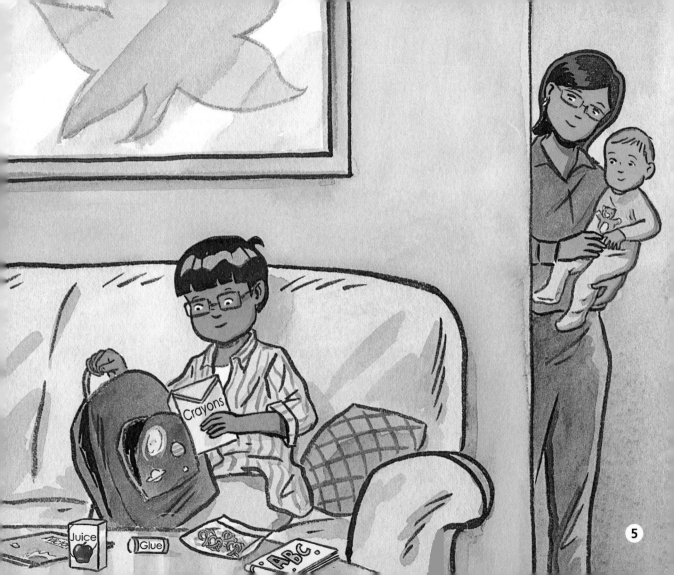

I pack my glue.

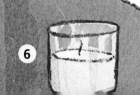

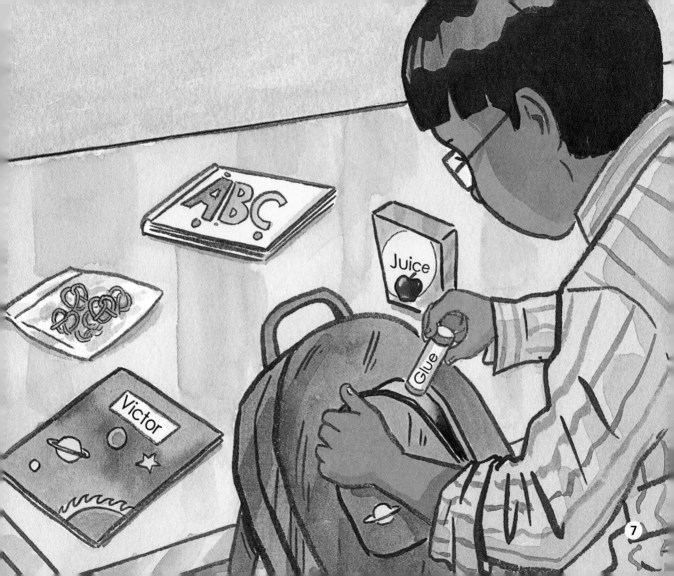

I pack my folder.

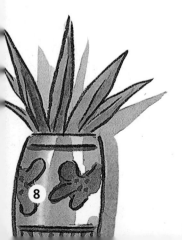

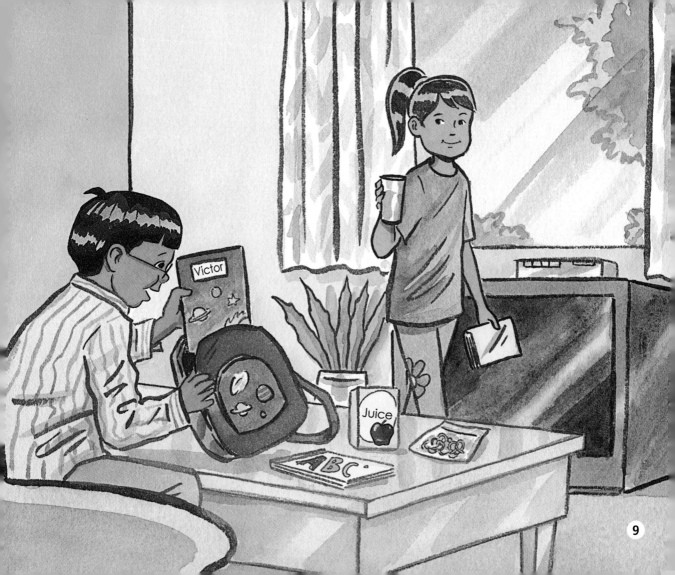

I pack my book.

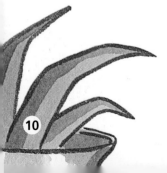

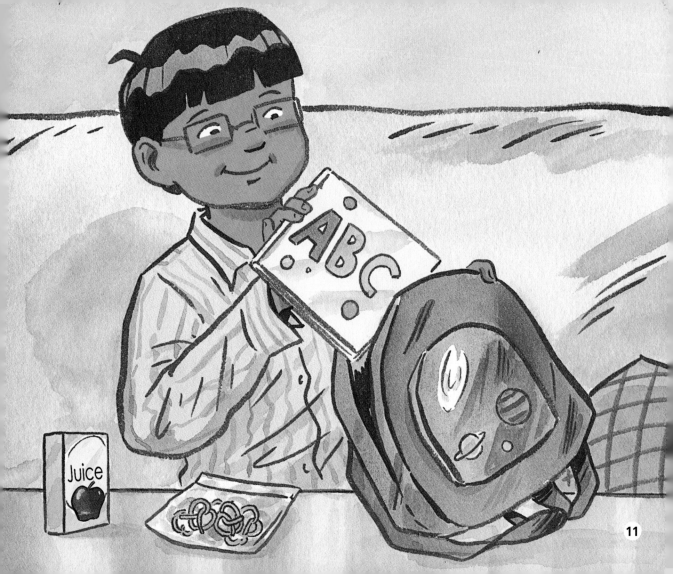

I pack my snack.

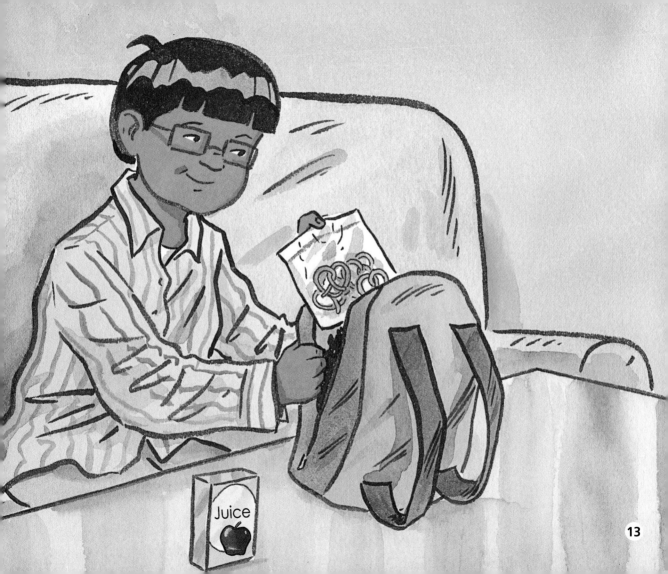

I pack my juice.

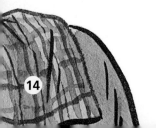

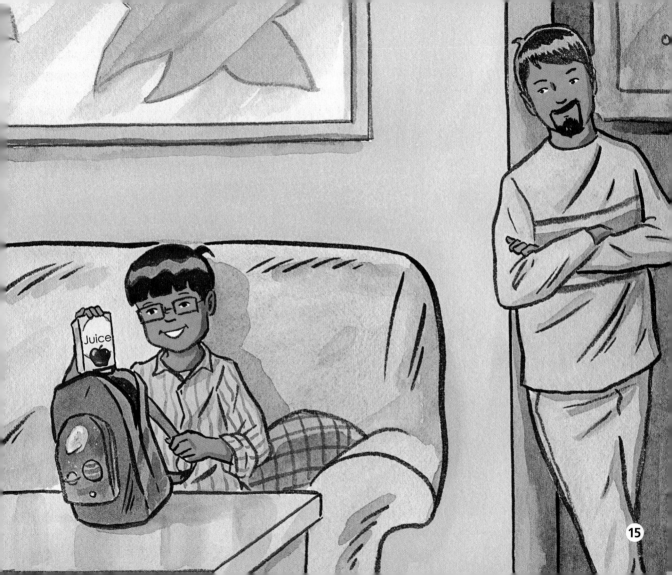

I packed my bag!

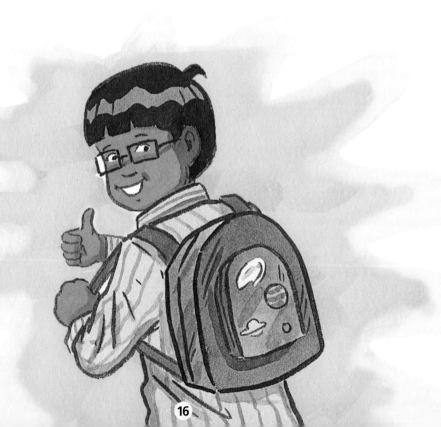